Sex With Strangers, The Collection

C. C. Passions

Published by Tales of Flesh Press, 2014.

SEX WITH STRANGERS, THE COLLECTION

First edition. March 11, 2014.

Copyright © 2014 C. C. Passions.

ISBN: 979-8201894788

Written by C. C. Passions.

Also by C. C. Passions

The Courier Guy, Sex With Strangers
Sex With Strangers, The Collection
Sex With Strangers, Triple Pack 1
Sex With Strangers, Triple Pack 2
Sex With Strangers, Triple Pack 3
Sex With Strangers, Triple Pack 4
The Book Store Babe, Sex With Strangers
The Busty Maid, Sex With Strangers
The Stranded Stranger, Sex With Strangers
Fun In The Garden, 2 Girls 1 Guy
Office Affair, 2 Girls 1 Guy
Room Mates, 2 Girls 1 Guy
Special Delivery, 2 Girls 1 Guy
The Cambodian Concubine
2 Girls 1 Guy, The Collection
2 Girls 1 Guy, Triple Pack 1
2 Girls 1 Guy, Triple Pack 2
2 Girls 1 Guy, Triple Pack 3
2 Girls 1 Guy, Triple Pack 4
Hot & Horny, Complete Edition
Hot & Horny, Mixer 1
Hot & Horny, Mixer 2
Hot & Horny, Mixer 3

Hot & Horny, Mixer 4
Erotic Mega Bundle
Hardcore Super Pack
Hot & Horny Mega Bundle
Adults Only, Quick & Dirty
Stained Sheets, Quick & Dirty
Filthy Fun, Hot & Horny
Taboo Temptation, Quick & Dirty

Table of Contents

The Courier Guy

(Sex With Strangers)

"I've had it with cheating men!" cried Tammy into her cell phone.

Her friend, Linda, who was on the receiving end of this declaration, tried to calm her down. "Oh, Tammy, honey," she said. "They're not all bad. Some of them are genuinely cowed enough to know they shouldn't mess with alpha females like us."

Neither woman felt such a statement was close to the truth, but it certainly helped Tammy a little to think it was. At least for the moment. Was she ready to give up on men all together?

Tammy paced her apartment living room. "I don't care to find out anymore. So many games, so many lies. A woman can't get anything honest from someone who owns a penis. They just can't be trusted."

She had reason to be angry. Andre, her boyfriend... ex-boyfriend... had just admitted to her, not fifteen minutes ago, that he had been unfaithful to her for the last two months of their relationship. With some waitress at a bar he frequented.

The coward had told her over the phone, too. He didn't have the nerve, or the balls, to tell her to her face. She would have liked to have punched him! Or at least scratched his eyes out.

Linda continued to try and calm her friend down. "Yeah, they're scum. They can't be trusted. Maybe you should just, I dunno, maybe take a break from serious relationships for a little bit. I know this just happened and all, but maybe this was for the best."

Tammy had paced into the bedroom and caught her reflection in the closet mirror. She was still in a bathrobe, having showered in preparation for going out with Carl that evening. She gave her body an appraising once over. She was hot dammit! Why would any man in his right mind even entertain the idea of screwing around behind her back? Especially *this* lovely back! She turned and lifted up the robe exposing a very firm, and pleasantly shaped, tear drop ass.

No more of this honey-dew for him!

"I know, I know," Tammy said. "It just hurts. I thought we had something truly meaningful. But I guess it wasn't meaningful enough." She gave her own ass a smack and was pleased that it barely shook. "Maybe I should just pick up some random piece of meat at the bar and screw the hell out of it."

"Yes!" Linda shouted. "Nothing better than cheap meaningless sex with a stranger to help you get through times of trouble."

Just then the downstairs buzzer rang.

"Who's that?" asked Linda.

"Oh, shoot. I was expecting a package delivered today for work." Andre had called her right after she got the a call-confirmation, asking if she would be home. She buzzed in whoever it was without answering.

"Wait a second, sister," said Linda, conspiratorially. "What if he's a hunk?"

Tammy scoffed. "No, it's always this little fat guy who smells of sweat and cheese."

"You should *do* him!"

"No way!" Tammy shuddered. Just the thought of it made her skin crawl.

"Or, it could be someone different. A moonlighting underwear model."

Tammy's brow furrowed. "Wow, you have quite the imagination. Well, if that were the case, he'd get one hell of a tip outta me, tonight."

"That a girl!" cried Linda.

Tammy was only half joking. It would take a lot to get her to indulge in a casual quickie with a stranger.

There was a knock at the door. Tammy took a moment to look herself over in the living room mirror. The robe hung half open, so she synched it closed. It accentuated her voluptuous breasts. Her muscular legs were bare for all to see. The robe only just covered her ass. She hadn't put on any underwear after she finished showering, and there certainly wasn't any time now to put some on.

I do look damn sexy, though, she thought to herself. At least mister chubby from the pizza place will get a little bit of an eye full.

While she walked to the door, Linda was chanting in the phone, "Hot sex! Hot sex! Hot sex!"

Tammy could only roll her eyes. As if.

She peered through the peek hole.

A tall dashing hunk of a man was standing out there. Holding a boxed package. Her boxed package.

"Uh," was all Tammy was able to say.

Linda immediately pounced. "What? WHAT?!"

Tammy found herself whispering, her eye glued to the hole, drinking in the beefcake outside. "It's not the usual guy. He's…" *Gorgeous.*

"So? Is he handsome, or just handsome enough?" asked Linda, intrigued with her friend's change of tone. "Either will do for now."

Tammy realized she had been staring at him entirely too long. She took a deep breath and opened the door.

The peephole view did not do this walking Greek God justice. Tall, chiseled features, and perfectly muscled, he gave Tammy a pearly white smile.

"Hi," he said. "I have a package delivery for a Tammy?"

Tammy was momentarily speechless. She was also alarmed to feel a dampness grow between her upper thighs.

"Yeah," she managed to stammer smiling, still a little shocked. She stepped back, letting him inside. She closed the door behind him.

She had forgotten her cell phone was in her free hand, until she dimly heard Linda cry out: "Do him! Screw his brains out! Give him a tip he'll never forget!"

Tammy quickly hung up. The delivery boy… man… stud, crooked a questioning eyebrow. She managed not to blush. "My friend is being annoying," she finally said, and immediately felt ridiculous.

He continued smiling politely, "Our delivery service has that effect on folks." His eyes were an incredible piercing blue, and they glanced down at her robe, and then at her legs before quickly returning to her eyes again.

She was surprised to find herself thrilled at this.

"You're not the usual courier guy."

"Oh, you probably get Peter," his voice was deep, confident. The kind you wouldn't mind having whispering instructions in your ear. "He called in sick so I had to pick up the slack."

She nodded, dully. This guy was a lot to take in. She suddenly found herself wondering just how much that would be, and in how many positions. "I've never seen you before. Are you new there?"

"New? Oh, more than that. I'm the owner."

She looked down at the company name on the package. It said Jim's Package Delivery Service. "You're Jim?" she said, incredulous.

"The big boss man himself," he said with a confident grin.

She found she was most definitely horny, now. Maybe there was a package he could delivery for her, and not the one in his hands.

She was struck with a strong impulse and felt an overwhelming urge to act on it. Linda was right. Meaningless sex with a stranger could be exactly what she needs right now. Especially with this particular handsome stranger.

"Oh, uh, please bring it in the living room," she said, walking away from him. He more or less had to follow. As she turned she sneaked a look at his wedding finger. Barren.

Good.

She also noted his eyes fell on her butt as she talked to him over her shoulder.

"Right over there, please," she pointed at the big coffee table which was between the couch and the easy chair. There was a plate of warmed up pizza she was nibbling on, sitting on the table.

Jim gave a short nod to her as he passed. She inhaled his wake as he did so, and liked the hint of his cologne, and the slight tinge of sweat. Most likely from working hard most of the night.

She yearned to make him sweat some more.

He placed the package on the table, and as he turned toward her, she quickly undid her robes, and let them fall to the floor. She put her hands on her curvy hips and bent a knee slighting for enticing emphasis.

He froze, eyes locked on her naked form. She was sexy as all hell, and she could see he thought the same.

"Well, Jim of Jim's Delivery Service," she said, with fire in her eyes, and a seductive

tone in her voice. "I have a way I can pay you properly for that package."

His jaw dropped, and his eyes roved over her. He was appropriately shell shocked, and took several moments to compose himself.

Who could blame him?

"I, uh…" he stammered.

Deciding to take her initiative even further she didn't want him to have to decide on his own. She walked forward, breasts jiggling hypnotically, and grabbed at his t-shirt. He only flinched just slightly, as if his brain was only now catching up with unfolding events, but he smiled and yielded.

He chuckled and raised his arms so she could pull the it off of him.

His chest did not disappoint. Ridged muscles lined his body and stomach. His pectorals were the size of dinner plates and his arms were hard as tempered steel, and almost as thick as her own thighs.

Tammy ran her hands over his barrelled chest. "You lift a lot of heavy packages to get a body like that?" she asked teasingly.

"Something like that," he said. His hands rubbed her shoulders, and up and down her arms. Then he cupped her ample breasts, squeezing them. She found his hands were calloused and strong, just the way she liked them.

She grabbed at his belt and undid it with a playful grunt. He smiled and let her work at it. When unbuckled, she unzipped his fly, then squatted down in front of him, pulling his pants down. She managed to work them to his hips, and with one final tug, yanked them down to his knees.

It was then that a huge dick popped out of them, partially engorged. The sudden motion of the pants had freed this large piece of meat from its lair, and it swung out and hit her in the side of the nose.

"Oh, my God!" She gasped. He smiled down at her. She blinked in astonishment. "I don't remember ordering this!" She giggled, amazed.

"It's an extra service. For hot, sexy customers only," he said.

She pulled off his shoes, and then aided him in removing his pants from his ankles. She then turned her attention to the now large erect penis in front of her, demanding attention.

Grabbing it eagerly, she stroking it up and down, marvelling at its thickness, and heft. Stealing her courage, she then put it in her mouth, and started to suck. It was large, but she had managed this size before.

Jim sighed with the sudden feel of her warm wet mouth on his prick, and the feel of her lips moving up and down his shaft. Because of his size, the sound of her slurping and occasional gagging was more prominent.

Up and down she worked him. Long minutes of concentrated effort, with her mouth made his dick glisten with her spit, creating a slight foam at its base. Some spit eventually dribbled down to his balls to dangle there in an elastic string.

Satisfied she had properly welcomed him into her home, she leaned back a bit for a breather, and gasped.

She motioned to the easy chair, "Sit down. I have an idea."

"I like your ideas so far," he said with wide appreciative eyes. He did as he was told.

She turned to the still-hot pizza slice on the table and stuck her fingers in it. As she tried to pick at a ring of green pepper she squealed girlishly from its heat. Finding one that suited her needs, she turned towards him, and his eyes widened at what she had in mind.

Gingerly, she broke it at one point, then wrapped the green pepper around the base of his thick cock. Because he was so well shaved, it rested against his skin and he hissed slightly, but not with great pain.

"You okay?" she asked coyly.

"Oh, yeah," he said through gritted teeth. "I knew my customers were hot but not *this* hot."

She grinned up at him, then swirled her tongue around his prick. She took his dick in her mouth, and slowly worked her way down his length, occasionally pausing to wiggle her head back and forth to help it past the hook at the back of her throat. He gasped, as her tongue poked out of the bottom of her gaping mouth. His girth had forced her mouth wide, stretching her lips around him. Spittle gathered in sticky strands at the corners.

With amazing patience, she neither gagged, or pulled back. She gazed up at him with big eyes, and her tongue prodded the green pepper until she managed to catch it. Then, very slowly, she slid back up his length, green pepper in tow.

Sucking him at the tip, the green pepper dangled from her mouth. Then she leaned back, plucking it in her fingers and smiling at him triumphantly.

"Impressive!" He said, laughing. "My turn to do a trick."

He eased her up off her knees, and had her sit in the easy chair, this time. She spread her legs by hooking her knees over the arms, exposing her very well shaved, and *very* wet pussy to him. She rubbed at her clit playfully.

"Do as you please, delivery boy," she said while teething the tip of one of her fingers.

"Oh, I will," Jim returned. With one finger he dipped into the tomato sauce of the pizza slice. Careful to get enough, he then slowly spread it around her pussy, smearing it completely with sauce.

It was her turn to grit her teeth from the heat, as he worked his fingers around her clit. Then he leaned forward, and with strong hands firmly holding her legs wide at the thighs, he started to lick.

Up and down, then all around, he licked and slurped. When a little sauce dripped down into the slight hollow at her asshole, he slurped it up. He then stayed there, rimming her asshole with his tongue.

Tammy gasped with pleasure, squeezing her tits, pinching at their erect nipples.

Then he returned his attention to her pussy, taking long deliberate licks, making sure he wasn't finished until it was completely cleaned of tomato sauce.

Jim grinned up at her and said, "My special sauce never tasted so damn good."

She smiled back and said, "Glad to finally be on your menu."

He then stood, cock hard and ready. He leaned forward, so he was hovering over her, and bent his dick as far as it would go. He stuck his prick into her waiting pussy. She gasped, and grabbed onto his hips. He paused, and said, "Can I make an express delivery, ma'am?"

"Please do!" Tammy said.

And with that, he suddenly slammed the entire length of his long dick deep inside her. She gasped with the hard penetration. He then lifted his ass up again, so his entire length was nearly unsheathed from her, and slammed it down again.

Over and over he did this, getting faster and faster. She moaned with each pelvic thrust. Long wonderful minutes passed as he slammed her pussy again and again. Eventually, the intensity got to be so much Tammy's eyes rolled upwards showing only their whites.

He reached around her neck and pulled against her head slightly, so as to cut off some of the circulation. She gasped for air while he continued his relentless hammering. He eased off her head only when she seemed close to passing out.

Then he slowed, making easy gyrating motions with his hips. Jim wanted to give her a little time to recover before giving her what was about to happen next.

When she seemed okay, he slipped out of her and her pussy gave a wet fart. He then turned her around and pushed her on the chair so her upper body leaning against the back of it. Her beautiful tits hung down over the back edge. Jim perched behind her, and smacked her incredible ass. It shook only slightly, being so firm.

Then he eased his dick into her pussy again, which was now sopping wet. Making sure Tammy was firmly pressed up against the chair, hands holding her hips tightly, he began to pump back and forth. Each time he slammed her ass she grunted with the force of it. He could feel the bottom of his cock rub hard against the inside of her and he knew she felt it, too.

Again, he was relentless in his pounding. Over and over. She gasped and moaned and dug her fingers into the chair. She was almost certain he was going to pound her straight through it.

The apartment filled with the ceaseless smacking of flesh on flesh. Punctuated with their moans of pleasure.

Eventually, he grabbed her arms, and pulled them back by the elbows, forcing her to arch her back. Her long blonde hair dangled down to almost brush against the small of her back, and shook with each hard thrust. He began to slam against her even harder and she moaned more deeply.

On the other side of the living room was a mirror. In the reflection, he could see her firm breasts moving with the harsh pounding rhythm. Her mouth was open, eyes were closed, and her brow was furrowed with gritting pleasure.

Over and over; again and again jim tapped that ass, until he could see that she was getting red where their flesh smacked against one an other.

He could not keep up this relentless pace. With both the feeling of him rubbing wetly inside her, and seeing her wonderfully firm flesh vibrating with his effort, he found himself about to explode.

"I'm gonna cum!" he practically shouted.

Quickly, Tammy pulled her body forward so as to unsheathe his dick from her, and she spun around. He stood, stroking his cock vigorously. She placed the bottom of her open mouth against the base of his prick. Her tongue tickled at it eagerly, and her eyes stared up at him with hunger.

He stroked faster, and soon exploded with a loud moan. He semen spat out all over her; many hot squirts into her mouth which slid down her tongue and pooled at the back of her throat. Over her face in long sticky strands that splayed across her cheeks and forehead. In the corner of one eye, down her chin, and he even got some in her blonde hair.

As he sagged with completion, she made a dramatic show of swallowing.

She smacked her mouth, and rolled her tongue around her lips, getting every white bit. A long thick strand still hung from her chin as she grinned widely at him.

She then grabbed his dick again, and sucked it as his erection faded, nursing the last of his load. She wanted every little bit of that special sauce.

It was while she was doing this, and looking up at the exhausted pleasure in his face, that she made a wondrous conclusion:

She needed to get courier service more often, dammit!

END

The Stranded Stranger

(Sex with Strangers)

Kimberly faced a long, and boring drive through the countryside as she headed south to visit family for the holidays.

She found the radio annoying as it continuously played sappy love songs over and over, so she just turned off. Unfortunately, this left her with her thoughts and memories of her recently failed relationship with her ex-husband, Martin. They had been married for less than three years but she knew it had been doomed from the start. The passion that initially attracted them to each other faded quickly and they simply fell into the routine of having each other around.

And it was passion she wanted more of in her life, and since there was no more with Martin she made the painful decision of cancelling the whole thing. They separated only last month and filed the divorce paperwork. And despite being amicable it was still quite stressful.

The early morning sun gave an orange hew to the sky, and tinged the countless trees that strobe by her on both sides of the winding country road. There was very little traffic, which was why she purposely took this more scenic route to her parents house several states away. She did not mind peacefulness but having Martin around for so many years she found a lack of another person's presence daunting.

She had no one else in her life at the moment to fill the void. Neither she nor Martin were unfaithful to the other during their failing relationship. And having only just recently separated she had neither the time, nor the will to find someone.

What she really craved with someone to find her. A distraction of the momentary kind. She did not think she had the emotional toolkit to deal with anything too heavy.

"I just need a man," she said to herself. She laughed at the absurdity of that declaration. She wasn't gonna find anyone at her parent's house, that was for certain. And she sure as hell didn't think anyone was waiting for her out here, in the middle of nowhere.

She peered up at the mountains, each covered with an apron of thick forest, that she slowly past by. "Nope," she said. "Only thing out here are mountain men and Bigfoot. And both would be too smelly for my taste."

As her mind wandered, she concentrated less on the road. At a particularly sharp turn, a figure suddenly appeared directly in front of her. A *man*, standing dangerously close to the edge of the turn in the road.

She yelped, and yanked at the wheel, swerving to avoid him. Her car fish tailed and she fought to control it. Pumping the brakes she managed to avoid flying off the road and into the trees. Always a cautious driver, she had not been travelling too fast and she skidded to a stop directly on the meridian facing the direction she had been coming from.

Her fingers were dug into the steering wheel and her hair was now in her face, which puffed out as she breathed heavily.

Is that what it's like to almost die?, she thought. She barked out a laugh, still in shock.

It was only after a few moments of recovering that she realized someone was running towards the car. The stupid guy!

Oh, I'm going to tear a strip out of him!, she thought as she released her vice like grip from the steering wheel, and pushed back her hair.

Her eyes widened in surprise as he got closer. *Sweet Lord,* she thought. *This guy looks like one of those underwear models you see on bus shelter poster ads. What the heck was he doing way out here?*

She found the wherewithal to roll down the window as he ran up to her driver's side door. His stunningly handsome face was only slightly marred by his expression of concern.

"What's an underwear model doing way out here?" she blurted. She put her hand to her mouth and she gasped at her own stupidity. "Was that my outside voice?"

He didn't seem to hear her, and said, "Are you all right? Are you hurt at all?" His voice was deep and husky. His light jacket emphasized his wide shoulders, and his jeans did little to hide his muscular thighs. For some bizarre reason his body reminded her of the trees all around, tall and strong.

Like a mountain man's!

"Yes," she finally managed to say. "I think I'm alive." She grinned up at him.

He sagged with relief, smiling for the first time, and she found his perfect teeth out did the brightness of the morning sun.

"Well, that's relief," he said, placing his hands on the rolled down window. She could not help but notice they were large and strong looking.

She caught herself wondering just how gentle those strong hands could be, moving up and down her body.

"I am so sorry," he said. "It was my fault. I didn't realize I was so close to the road. My car broke down." He hitched a thumb over at the little dodge parked on the road side.

"Oh, no, it was my fault," she said. "I wasn't paying attention, my thoughts drifted..." and as she said that she realized her drifting thoughts had been about a much needed man to distract her from her troubles. She looked up at his handsome face, with its chiseled features and strong jaw. *And I go ahead and nearly kill the only man for miles!*

"I can't get any reception on my phone," he said. "Could I use yours to call for a tow truck?"

"Sorry, but I don't have one," she said, sheeply.

"Ah, that's too bad," he said, disappointed. He was looking at her, smiling, when she had a thunderous revelation.

"Hey," she said sweetly. "Since I almost splattered you all over the road, the least I could do is offer you a ride." She felt her face reddening as she spoke, trying not make it obvious what kind of ride she really had in mind.

He arched a brow, considering the offer. Finally, he said, "Where are you headed?"

"South. A long way south, actually."

He frowned a little and she was momentarily mortified she would lose him. But again, he regarded her with that sexy arch of the eyebrow. "I think the next town is only a couple of miles further up the road." He shrugged as if to suggest he really didn't want to bother her any more.

Oh, he could bother her, alright.

She grinned. "I'll take you. It's the least I could do. It might keep me from running you over again when I turn around."

He laughed. "Okay. You win. Just let me grab my stuff." He trotted back to his car.

She watched the movement of his buttocks in his jeans as he moved.

Yum, yum, yum, she thought.

She turned the car around in a wide arch, to point back in the southerly direction she was original travelling. This time she didn't almost kill him.

She watched as he grabbed a duffle bag from the front seat, then locked the car. Her heart was pounding excitedly in her chest. She looked at herself in the rear view mirror, and made a vain attempt at fixing her tussled hair. She locked eyes with herself.

Do you know what you are doing girl?

She grinned. *Yes, I'm going to be doing him!*

He came back, and thru his bag in the backseat. Then he sat down in the passenger side, closing the door. As he settled in, she sneaked a peak at his crotch.

Yup, she thought, *he definitely has a penis*. With that confirmed, she now had to find out if he knew how to use it.

He turned and smiled at her, offering his hand.

"I'm Bob."

She took it, and tried not to shiver with the electric touch of him.

"Kimberly."

They shook.

Kimberly found she was unwilling to release is hand right away. But when he arched that brow again and added that cute smile, she relented. She pulled out on the road and drove, trying mightily to keep her eyes from staring at him.

They made very idle chit chat, of which none involved her getting naked, and him spanking her. She was just trying to work up the courage to make it happen. Yet, she got the distinct sense he was intrigued by her. Maybe even found her attractive.

It only took a few minutes but they arrived at the town turnoff. Her mind was racing. She had an impulse and by God she was going to see it through, this time! She slowed the car.

"Hey, what's that over there," she said pointing towards what looked like the entrance to an old dirt road that disappeared into the forest.

He looked. "Looks like a switchback road," he said. "Runaway truck use them in an emergency."

"Wow. I've never seen one of those maybe I'll go down a little ways just to check out. Would be nice and private." She looked at him meaningfully. "Care to come have an emergency with me?"

His eyebrows had raised in surprise making him look all the more adorable.

A second passed and then another, each feeling like years to Kimberly.

He chuckled slightly, then settled back in his seat. He then regarded her with a seductive smile. "That's a fantastic idea," he said.

She laughed.

Hoping not to lose him in the moment, she quickly steered the car onto the switchback road.

She drove slowly down the gravel road while fully conscious of the glances he was giving her. The moment the highway seemed a safe distance out of view, she pulled over as far as she could and parked, again.

She turned the car off, and killed the power, too, and sat back.

They both grinned nervously at each other.

"Well," Kimberly said. "What do we do now?"

Bob made a show of looking around at their surroundings. "I dunno. Is this the spot you normally take the men you almost run over?"

She laughed, undid her seat belt, and moved over to him closing the distance. Placing a hand on his strong shoulder she whispered in his ear, "Yes, and I would like to suck your cock, as an apology." To ensure he did not miss her meaning, she grabbed the bulge in his jeans. She was happy to note that it was already growing in size.

"Yes, ma'am!" he said, and leaned back to undo his belt. She helped him. When it was undone he eased his hips forward so she would have room.

She fished his dick out of its hiding place, it was firm and erect. She kissed the tip several times, feeling its throbbing heat in her hand. Gently, she started to lick its length, up and down from the base of his shaft to the swollen prick. Like a lollipop.

He gasped softly, putting one hand on the back of her head to guide her up and down movements.

He then reached down, found the release for the chair and angled it back some more, giving her more room to work on him properly.

With his knob glistening from her diligent licking, she then took his fat prick into her mouth, pushing it up to the back of her throat as far as it would go. Her lips firmly gripped his shaft as they moved closer to the base, her nose touched his stomach.

Then she sucked at it, moving her head up and down all the way. She stroked him with her hand, following it with her lips.

He groaned.

For several long wonderful minutes she sucked his cock, until he reached a point she was certain he was going to shoot his load. The car filled with sound of her hard sucking, and hungry slurping.

Carefully, she slowed, not wanting him to be spent too soon. Kissing the tip of his prick on more time, she then looked up at him with a big smile.

She said, "Let's fuck."

He smiled back, but offered that cute arching brow again. "It's a little crowded in here for that, don't you think?"

She sat up a little and said, "Well, you are a big boy. Let's take this party outside."

And with that they jumped out of the car. Before he moved around towards he she pointed at him and commanded, "Strip Mister!"

He laughed, but did as he was told, stripping his clothes off, his hard on quivering with each motion.

She did the same, deftly peeling off all her clothing in under a minute. They threw their clothes into the car. The gravel felt cool under her feet.

Bob walked quickly around to her side of the car, holding his stiff dick.

"I want you to fuck me this way," she said, motioning for him to get in back of her.

She stood standing with her arms braced, one against the open door, the other against the car roof. She spread her legs out a little and stuck her butt out, arching her back.

He smacked her ass, and moved up behind her. Holding his dick he rubbed its prick along the inside folds of her pussy, exploring her wetness, teasing her with it.

When she could no longer stand the anticipation commanded, "Fuck me! Just fuck me, dammit!"

"Okay," he said, and suddenly lunged forward, jamming the entire length of him inside her with one motion.

She gasped, and gritted her teeth as he immediately started to pound against her. Her braced arms tensed with each impact. She delighted in knowing that if she hadn't held herself in such a way, he may very well of fucked her straight through the door with his powerful thrusts.

He pounded against her, over and over, until her moans grew louder and more intense. Her flesh grew red where he smashed up against her. He smacked her ass repeatedly, slapping each one in turn.

As he continued to fuck her, he licked his thumb and then rubbed it against her little ass-hole. He circled it with his thumb over and over.

Several minutes passed as he worked on her, and the forest filled with the sounds of their passionate efforts. She moaned, and occasionally yelped when he smacked her reddening flesh. He gasped, trying desperately not to cum just yet.

When he was close to being spent he slowed, easing in and out of her gently. He reached up and cupped her tits, which were perky and firm. He squeezed them, and pinched at her erect nipples.

Then, he pulled out of her, and smacked her ass loudly one more time.

"Ow!" she cried with delight.

"I want to eat your pussy," he said pointing towards the hood of the car.

She glowed. "Great idea!"

She giggled as she tiptoed to the front of the car. He followed in hot pursuit. The hood was sloped and she eased herself up it by wiggling her bum. Then she leaned back on her elbows and spread her legs.

The fibreglass popped and sagged with her weight.

"I don't think this car was designed for this," she said, not caring in the least.

"Let's see what else it wasn't designed for," he said with mischievous smile. He squatted in front of her, placing those strong hands against her widened thighs, then he leaned forward and gave her shaved pussy a nice long welcoming lick.

Then he licked again, and again, until he developed a rhythm. Kimberly bent her head back and smiled gloriously up at the blue morning sky, enjoying the sensation of his tongue all over her pussy.

Eventually, he sucked on one of his fingers to get it wet, then he cautiously slipped it up inside her, and she gasped. Then he started to make a come-hither motion against the sensitive pad just behind her pubic bone. She shivered with pleasure, practically seeing stars before her eyes with the intensity.

He returned to work, concentrating more now on her clit. He sucked at it, tickling it with his tongue at the same time. All the while, she gasped with pleasure, squeezing her tits, pinching at their erect nipples. She took one in her mouth and teethed it, sucking.

He ate her out for long moments, listening to the wet sounds his gyrating finger made inside her.

When he had his fill he then stood, cock hard and ready. He leaned forward, so he was hovering over her, and bent his dick as far as it would go. He stuck his prick into her waiting pussy. She gasped, and grabbed onto his hips.

"You want this?" he asked.

"Yes!" she begged. "Fuck the hell outta me!"

And with that, he suddenly slammed the entire length of his long dick deep inside her. She gasped with the hard penetration. He then lifted his ass up again, so his entire dick was nearly unsheathed from her, and slammed it down again.

The hood of the car popped and squawked with the hard pressured movements.

Over and over he did this, getting faster and faster. She moaned with each pelvic thrust. Long wonderful minutes passed as he slammed her pussy again and again. Eventually, the intensity got to be so much Kimberly's eyes rolled upwards, completely lost in the rapture of the moment.

Over and over; again and again he slammed down onto her.

He could not keep up the relentless pace. With both the feeling of the rubbing wet friction inside her, and seeing her face grimace with the concentrated effort of their passion, he found himself about to orgasm.

"I'm gonna cum!" he finally shouted.

Quickly, Kimberly pushed him back, unsheathing him form her.

He stood before her, stroking his cock vigorously. Sitting on the edge of the hood, she leaned forward so she could place the bottom of her open mouth against the base of his prick. Her tongue tickled at it eagerly, and her eyes stared up at him with hunger.

He stroked faster, and soon came with a loud moan. His semen spat out all over her; hot squirts into her mouth which slid down her tongue and pooled at the back of her throat. Over her face in long sticky strands that splayed across her cheeks and forehead. In the corner of one eye, down her chin, and he even got some in her hair.

As he sagged with completion, she made a dramatic show of swallowing.

She smacked her mouth, and rolled her tongue around her lips, getting every white bit. A long thick strand still hung from her chin as she grinned widely at him.

She then grabbed his dick, and sucked it as his erection faded, nursing the last of his load.

Looking up at his handsome face, seeing the sunshine glint off the sweat on his muscular chest, she came to a conclusion:

She needed to almost run over hunks more often!

END

The Book Store Babe

(Sex With Strangers)

Andre loved books almost as much as he loved sex. Almost.

Yet, he never thought the two would actually collide together until he met the cute new employee at the book store.

He had been going to that store for many years. Occasionally, there would be an attractive clerk working there. Usually, it was someone who primarily stocked shelves with all the new releases. The work itself required lots of kneeling, stretching and bending.

When one of these cuties worked in his area, he found that sitting in one of the lounge chairs gave him a good view of their comings and goings.

Sadly, though, there seemed to be a high turnaround at the store. Whether to internal staff politics, general attrition (he couldn't imagine doing that type of work for years) or they here migrated to other branches, he never knew. But many hot, and/or cute, (or both) shelf stockers simply vanished from his almost weekly appreciations.

Or maybe they left because of him? He'd often wondered how obvious he was when he sneaked glances at their bums as the sauntered past, or bent down to add some books (That was certainly his favourite part of their job!). Also, as they were lost in the mundane concentration of their work, the almost never realized he was staring at their breasts. Side boob view was another favourite. You may not get a full appreciation of breasts full on, masked by a sweater or baggy blouse. But turned to the side, the breast was particularly arousing.

Then one day, there was a new little brunette librarian. She was about his age, tiny in stature, but with a slim, yet very shapely figure. Thankfully, a lot of her books needed stocking right in front of where he was sitting.

Playing casual, he peeked at her from over the edge of his book, thus allowing him to ogle her magnificent butt. *Jeans were created to be worn by this girl*, he thought.

She had bent over, revealing the beautiful teardrop shape of her ass.

He felt himself getting hard, and he looked down at his crotch, making sure everything was still in order and not bulging out at a revealing angle.

"Found what you are looking for?" asked a pleasant female voice.

He looked up, and blanched. It was her. The brunette cutie was standing directly in front of him.

What did she mean? Looking for my boner? A book? Her?

"Uh," was all he could manage in that moment of shock. He became frighteningly aware of bulge growing bigger.

Did her eyes just flicker down at it? He thought, embarrassed. Maybe was she just looking at the book in his hand?

"Enjoying the selection?" she asked, with a crook of her eyebrow. Her expression seemed to show more than a passing interest in what his answer could be.

Was she flirting with him?

"Yeah, great selection. Thanks," he said. *Geez, could I sound more stupid?*

"I'm Sasha," she suddenly offered. "Just started here today."

He was a little tongue tied, not expecting to have to actually *interact* with this object of desire. *Who'd of thunk of such a concept?*

"A-Andre," he stammered. His heart was now thundering against his chest. Hopefully, his face didn't go red like it usually did when he was flustered.

"Well, A-Andre," she said with a smile and a wink. "Maybe I'll see you around?"

"Yeah, definitely," he said.

She turned to go, but paused. His heart stopped.

She nodded her head at his... crotch? At his growing hard on? He wanted to cross his legs but his erection would just make it look even funnier.

"By the way, you're reading it upside down," she grinned wickedly at him, and walked away, pushing the cart. He could have sworn she put in an extra bit of sway to those perfect hips.

He watched her leave, a bit in a daze. Looking at the book in his hands, he saw that she was right.

Stunned, he waited for his hard on to die down. He even managed to read a little of the book (right side up this time), until he felt he had embarrassed himself enough for one day.

He was walking towards the exit when he suddenly heard something.

"A-Andre!" someone hissed from behind. He turned and was struck dumb when he saw that it was Sasha. She was leaning around the end of a bookshelf, out of sight of the front door cash register. She peeked down towards the cashier then, looking back at him, waved his hand at him, indicating he should come over.

Thankfully, his legs took the initiative and propelled him to her, before his brain could screw things up.

When he got close, and obviously wasn't moving fast enough for her, she grabbed his arm and pulled him behind the shelves. Her firm touch electrified his bare skin. He found himself grinning.

She grinned back. "Got a question for you, A-Andre." she said, looking quite beautiful.

"Okay," was all he could say.

"Wanna fuck my brains out?"

His breath caught.

Oh.

My.

God.

His brain had seized up. Miraculously, he found himself nodding.

Pleased, she took his hand and quickly led him into a back storage room, which was filled with books, and boxes, from top to bottom. She closed the door behind them.

"Now, you're going to have to wait her until closing and everyone else leaves." She looked up at him with big wide stunning eyes that melted his heart and began to stiffen his crotch again. "Will you wait here for me, A-Andre?"

Duh.

Shrugging, he said, "Yeah, no problem, he said, casually. Like getting propositioned by store clerks was an everyday occurrence for him.

She nodded, but looked at him as if analyzing his honesty. "You know what?" she said.

"What?"

"Let me give you a little taste of what you can expect if you do stay."

Before he could say anything she dropped to her knees in front of him. His eyes widened, and his boner screamed to be released.

"Whip it out," she said.

There is a God! his brain seemed to cheer at him.

"Hurry," she said. "I'm only suppose to be on my coffee break." She looked up at him. "And I wanna little taste, too."

He had never unbuckled his belt, and undid his zipper, that fast before in his life. His erect dick practically popped out at her with the sudden motion of pulling down his pants past his waist.

She giggled a little, but immediately grabbed it. The warmth of her hand on his throbbing member, nearly made him cum right there, but he grit his teeth.

"Mmmm," she said. She very gently kissed the tip of his dick. "I like the taste of that." She stuck out her tongue and flickered it against his prick. She did this for several moments, alternating between kissing and flickering at it.

Then, suddenly, she opened her mouth wide and lunged forward. Nearly his entire cock was swallowed in one motion. He felt the top of his dick slide against the roof of her mouth, and lodge in the back of her hot throat.

He moaned.

"Mmmm," she said again. At least that's what it sounded like. She did have a big cock in her mouth, after all.

Clinching her lips around his girth, she began to move her head up and down. She sucked at him, gently.

Soon, the only thing he could feel was her determined grip at the base of his shaft and part of her palm against his balls, and the hot sensation of the wonderful wet friction of his member sliding in and out of her mouth.

He moaned again. He was now having a heck of a time not cumming and preventing hot jizz from exploding out of the back of her head.

"Sasha to the front cash! Sasha to the front cash!" suddenly said a loud voice.

They both froze.

It was the intercom.

But she didn't lose her cool. Slowly, almost deliberately, she slide up his shaft, which now was slick with her spittle. Her sucking lips slide over his prick, but remained locked on the very tip of it. As she looked up at him he felt her tongue flicker feather-like at the tip.

Then she pulled it out and gave it one last quick kiss. She stood, and he found himself standing in front of her holding his wet throbbing dick. *Was it over?*

"This is not over," she said, as if reading his thoughts. She stood on her tip toes and kissed him on the lips.

"I liked that taste, and I'll be back for more," she said. "Think you can wait for me?" She grinned evilly.

"Yeah!" he gasped. *Sweet Lord Almighty, Yes!*

And with that, she slipped out the door, and closed it behind her, locking it.

He was left standing there, pants down to his knees, holding his dick.

Not wanting to rub one out (gotta save that for later), he did up his pants, and spent the time reading while waiting.

It didn't take long. Soon, some of the lights went off, but a bank of them stayed on in the storage room. Closing time.

Then, after what seemed like forever, the door clicked open, and for a brief moment, he thought someone other than Sasha was going to come in and find him there.

It wasn't. Face beaming, Sasha entered, and relocked the door behind her.

"Well, well, well," she said. "Tired of waiting?"

He sprang to his feet from the chair he had been reading in. "Nope, not at all. Uh, are we alone now?"

She smiled. "Yes, and let me prove it." Suddenly, in one fluid motion, she pulled off her shirt. Andre was rendered speechless, as she was not wearing a bra (which he had suspected), and her small, perky breasts presented themselves to the world to be admired.

He also couldn't help but notice she had a flat, well defined tummy.

"Wow," he said.

"It gets better," with a couple of quick motions, she pulled down her jeans, as well as her thong panties, down to her ankles. She grinned at him as she kicked off her shoes, and stepped out of everything.

Eager to join in the festivities, Andre quickly pulled off his own shirt, and tossed it. Then he started on his pants, before she walked over to him, and put her hands on his belt buckle. His eyes were on the trim triangle of hair that was between her well muscled thighs.

"Wait, not yet," she said.

Certain he would do as she asked, she sashayed over to the desk. Andre' eyes were locked on that amazingly firm butt, and the tiny peek of a pussy they presented.

She glanced back at him, then bent straight over the desk, so her elbows were leaning on the top. Wiggling her ass, Andre could now see the well shaved pinkness of her pussy. "I want you to spank me," she said.

Transfixed by the movement of her naked flesh and that wondrous ass, he walked up behind her. Impulsively, he cupped her buttocks. *Sweet Nirvana!* He thought.

He wanted to fuck her so hard, right then and there, but decided to play along. Holding up a hand at the ready, he looked at her for his queue.

"Spank me," she said. So he did, with a light slap. First one cheek, and then the other. He really enjoyed how her firm buttocks moved when he did so.

She shuddered, and said, "Harder! And don't be a pussy about it!"

Well, okay then, he thought.

He did, this time a little harder, and using his full palm, not just the fingers. She yelped, and he found his hand actually stung.

"More!"

"Yes, Ma'am!" he said, and did so. Over and over he smacked her lovely ass, until it progressed to a full on spanking. Each time she yelped, or groaned. She even gritted her teeth to keep from screaming out, but that didn't last long as he kept at it. Smack, smack, smack.

She raised a hand. "Okay, okay," she panted. "Stop!"

Disappointed, he did. "Did I hurt you?" He hadn't wanted to have this kinky little exercise end due to him being overzealous.

"No," she said. "Not yet." She grinned evilly.

Andre nearly cam in his pants from her expression alone.

"Not yet?" he echoed, oblivious to the meaning, but wanting to know more, all the same.

She pointed to one of the carts, which was full of thick hardcovers. "Grab a classic."

Obeying, he walked over to it, feeling his hard-on chaff roughly against the inside of his pants. Not trying to be subtle, he shifted his dick over with one hand, as he picked out a book from the cart selection with the other.

"How about this?" he asked.

Her panting had lessened, and she was using a hand to reach around and massage her the bright red skin of her ass. "Is it a classic?"

"Classic?" he looked. "Uh, it's about medicine or something."

She had moved a finger over her raw pussy, and she flinched with ecstasy at the painful touch. "No, not that one. Get something good, something that has meaning."

Confused at the request, but not wanting to question it for fear of putting a sudden end to this wonderful encounter, he picked out another book.

"The Complete Dickens Collection," he said hefting the large tome. It was thick and weight a good couple pounds.

She nodded with a smile, one finger teasing the wetness of her pussy around. "That will do. It has Dick in it."

Andre actually laughed out loud. She laughed too.

He was not going to argue this, so he stood behind her, and to one side. *Fuck she looks hot*, he thought. She had braced her arms on the desk again, in preparation of the wonderful pain.

He gripped the big book with both hands, and hoisted it over one shoulder. This view accentuated the wonder curve of her buttock muscles, and again, his boner begged to be released.

"I'd really like to fuck the hell out you right now," he admitted. He almost regretted blurting it out, but God damn this chick looked fuckable as all hell.

She winked at him over shoulder, "Soon. Very, very soon. But first, do this to me. I need it to get going." She smiled.

God, I am one lucky guy, he thought. His face actually hurt from grinning so much.

"Ready?" he asked.

Without saying anything, she faced forward again, and nodded her head vigorously. She was psyching herself up.

She took a deep breath. He took a deep breath.

He swung hard aiming at the curving muscle of her ass, directly from behind.

She grunted, but gritted her teeth. And he smacked her again, then again. Over and over.

At first, she kept the noise she made to a minimum, but as he kept spanking her with the big book, she started to get louder. Soon, she was almost shouting with each and every smack.

Her body would even quiver with the anticipation of each hit. But she didn't tell him to stop. She only flinched, making her small pert breasts jiggle.

Eventually, she raised her hand again, and he stopped. She was breathing too hard from the shrieking to say anything at first. He lowered the book, and waited. His cock throbbed in his pants for her. She looked so damned fuckable.

"Okay, okay!" she was gasping. "Now get some Shakespeare!"

Was she kidding? When were they gonna fuck? He thought, incredulous. But he did as he was asked. When a hot, naked chick, who is bent over begging to be spanked and spanked hard, asks you to do something that turns her on even more; you did it, damn it!

He got it, and it was twice the size of the other. His eyes widened as he hefted it. "Are you sure?" he asked, concerned.

"Yeah," she said, nodding quickly. "Do it now before I change my mind! Spank my ass with it!"

Again, he smacked her, again she shrieked with pain and delight. He repeated this over and over until he was certain the bright red skin on her ass was going to burst from all that punishment.

This time, she did not last as long as previously before she raised her hand, and he stopped.

He found his fingers actually started to hurt, where they got caught between the book and the firm flesh of her ass. He could even see they made a couple of impressions on her lovely skin. Red on red.

She was gasping for air, and her whole body quivered and shoke. *Is she having an orgasm?* He thought.

"Okay," she said, gulping in air. "Pants off!"

He did not require any further coaxing, and his shoes, pants and boxers flew in different directions within seconds.

Bent over as she was, her pussy was pushed out, glistening. He could see she was very wet, to the point where it dribbled all down her lips, and partially down one of her inner thighs.

His mouth watered just looking at it.

"Eat me," she said. "Lick me all up."

All right! He got down on his knees, lightly gripped her red ass, spreading the rounded cheeks a little. Then he licked her; nice and long at first, from the bottom to the top. *Or was it top to the bottom from this angle?* he thought.

She tasted incredible and he told her so. Her pussy was sopping wet from being turned on so much from the spanking. He could feel the heat of the blood brought so close to the surface of her red skin, rubbing against his cheeks and chin. He licked her for several long tasty minutes until she was moaning again. He could feel her wetness all over his chin, and some dribbled a little down his throat.

Careful, he sucked out her clit between his lips, and it was his turn to use his tongue for flickering.

Sasha arched her back, groaning. Occasionally she pushed back so his face was forced deeper inside her incredible wetness, and he nearly went mad with the feeling of it.

He worked on her pussy like this for a long time, sucking up her lips so their soft folds slipped in gently between his teeth. Her entire body shuddered and quaked. Eventually, she couldn't handle any more, and said, "Fuck me!"

She looked over her shoulder at his eyes that peeked over the curvature of her ass. "Fuck me with your Dickens!"

He stood up, grabbed his dick (or was it Dickens?) which was now pulsating, and put his other hand on her ass. Then, very slowly, he slide his prick into her. He bite his bottom lip because he nearly lost it right there.

Taking a moment to gather himself, he then slid his entire length into her. He gasped. She felt so damn good; very hot, and very wet. Then he slid back his length until it was nearly out, and slammed it back in all the way. She grunted. He did it again. And again.

He pumped her, hard as she had asked him to. He marvelled at the the bright redness of her ass, and gazed down appreciatively at her little pink ass-hole. He rubbed at her asshole with a thumb, all the while not stopping with his rhythm. Her flesh jiggled, but was so firm it barely moved.

She tossed her head back and forth, occasionally arching her back all the way so he could reach around and squeeze her firm little tits. At one point he pulled her back by the elbows so she was almost standing up straight, and slammed her pussy harder and harder.

Soon, after all that had happened, and with the incredible sensation of being finally inside her, he couldn't hold it any longer.

"Ah, fuck!" he groaned loudly.

She instinctively knew what this meant, reached back and gently pushed at his stomach so he eased out of her. Her pussy made wet noises as if in protest.

Spinning around, she dropped to her knees in front of him, and as he stroked his shaft, she slurped his dick into her hot mouth. She sucked furiously until he practically screamed as he came into her mouth.

Somehow she managed to chuckle while sucking him off. His hips bucked with his orgasm, as if he was fucking her mouth. When he was nearly spent, she swallowed loudly, never letting his cock out of her mouth. He sagged against the desk as she continued to nurse his load.

"Whoa," he said. He could feel his body was covered in sweat from such wonderful exertion.

She pulled his cock out of her mouth with a wet pop, and said, "Well, A-Andre. Thanks for the quickie. This really topped off my day." She smiled and returned to sucking him dry.

Chuckling, Andre couldn't agree more!

END

The Busty Maid

(Sex With Strangers)

When Kevin answered his front door, the stunning young woman standing outside literally rendered him speechless.

She was blonde, young, and amazingly curvy; like a walking hourglass. But what really caught his gaze was her incredible bosom. Big breasts that seemed to be nearly bursting out of the skin tight t-shirt she wore.

My God, he suddenly thought, *those must be forty-four double-dees!*

Thanks to her youthful age, her breasts easily defied gravity by barely sagging.

"Hi," she said, cheerfully. "I'm Annette. The house cleaning agency sent me. Are you Kevin?"

Man the torpedoes, he thought. *She must stack those on shelves at night.*

His mouth dropped, but managed to gather his senses and say, "Oh, yes. I am. Please come in." He stood back and she walked past him into the foyer. He got a nice whiff of her perfume, and repressed a shudder.

"Nice place you have," she said. As she looked around, he sneaked a glance at her legs. She was wearing very short shorts, that only came down to her upper thigh. If this was a standard issue maid uniform then he was an instant fan. Her legs were muscular and tanned. He wondered how smooth they would feel if he ran his hands over them.

She looked back at him, "So, where would you like me to start?"

"Uh, yeah. Right," he said, barely managing to tear his gaze from hers. She was watching him rather intensely.

"Well, you can start wherever you like. It's a big house and is quite the handful."

"Are you?" she asked, one cute eyebrow bending in question.

"Am I what?"

"A handful?" her smile turned into a grin.

Holy shit, he thought. *Is this little goddess actually flirting with me?*

Still, she grinned at him, and that eyebrow remained crooked.

No, he thought. *She's just teasing me. I'm so out of practice with women my hopes have started to blur reality. No way as young and hot as this would be into a middle aged frump like me.*

She turned and looked around. Kevin got a side profile of those breasts, and that incredible bouncy ass, which nearly caused him to faint.

"I'll start with the upstairs," she said. "Then I'll work my way down slowly." She eyed him. "Always works for me."

"Okay," Kevin said, trying to regain his senses and not make a fool of himself. "I have to go meet a friend for a bit. Should be back in a couple of hours."

She gave him that wicked grin again, and said, "Oh, don't have to much fun now."

He left the house, feeling like all he really wanted to do was stay home and watch her glide around. *Ah well*, he thought to himself. *Some young buck must be tapping that without any appreciation of just how God damned lucky his his. Little bastard.*

He drove across town to his favourite watering hole, The Richman's Pub. After parking in his usual spot he went inside to find that his drinking buddy, George had already arrived. He had claimed a table near the waitress serving section of the bar, where the pretty servers line up to get their orders. Making for nice viewing while they chatted.

"Hey, what's up?" George said. He had one eye on his depleting beer, and the other on the backside of one of the waitress standing across from them.

"I should be asking you that," said Kevin with grin.

"Nothing that the ladies can't be taught to handle," said George, and they both laughed. "So, anything new in the wonderfully dull world that is Kevin?" George had always teased him about woeful lack of dating since his divorce. Kevin just wasn't ready, George felt it was his obligation as a single male, to go forth and get into the panties of any female that would let him.

"Well, you're not gonna believe this, but I met a woman."

George leaned forward, suddenly intrigued. "Oh, share with me buddy, who is she?"

"The new maid."

"The new maid? Oh, wow. Robbing the cradle?" he grinned.

Kevin held up his hands, "Nah, she's twenty or so, she's not really a kid."

"That makes it all the better, dear boy!"

They stopped talking so as to smile at the cute waitress who dropped off Kevin's beer. Their eyes were on her ass as she walked away, then clinked their glasses together in mutual appreciation.

George raised an eyebrow at him. "Well, tell me. What does this maid look like?"

So Kevin described her in minute detail, sparing nothing. He sounded like a teenager with his lewd language, but he was with his friend, and guys always talked that way. Especially when there wasn't any females around to protest.

But when he described Annette's most noticeable assets, her breasts, George's face dropped.

"Wait," George said, "That sounds familiar. She's from a cleaning service?"

"Yeah," Kevin tried to hide the concern in his voice. Why would Annette be familiar to George?

Suddenly, George threw his head back and laughed. "Oh, man that is rich! You are one lucky son of a bitch, you know that?"

"What? Why?"

"Let me guess, is her name Annette?"

Kevin was dumbstruck. "Yeah, Annette. How the hell did you know?"

George was still laughing, tears rolling down his face.

"Come on, tell me, dammit!" said Kevin, growing very annoyed.

George settled down, and when he stopped laughing he looked at Kevin with a big, shit eating grin. "Buddy, you hit the jackpot. Remember Richard? That guy we played golf with during the summer?"

"Yeah, so?"

"Well, he told me about this hot as hell blonde maid he once hired, who had tits to die for. Her name was Annette, too."

"No, way. Can't be the same one."

"I don't doubt that it is. I mean what are the odds. Same hair, same age, same body, same general neighbourhood. And most importantly, same giant gravity defying tits!"

Kevin felt himself growing disappointed. "So, what happened?"

George sipped his beer, "What do think what happened? The fucked like rabbits."

"I don't believe it."

"Oh, it's true alright. And she was a complete sex fiend, too. The best kind. She'd come over, and he'd leave to run some errands. Then, when he came back they'd fuck. And fuck a lot, from what I remember him saying."

"Really?"

"He said she'd ride him all night, and suck him dry. Suck him dry! Now where can I get a girl like that?" George grinned. "Oh, I know. At your place."

"Okay, settle down. Fine, so what if it's her. They still a couple?"

George almost spat out a mouthful of beer, "Hell no. Purely sexual. The best kind there is, as we both know. Just wanted him for the sex. But, they stopped a while ago."

"Why's that?"

"On account of he got married to some brunette from his office. Now he uses a different maid, some old woman who looks like a Russian shot-putter." George shrugged. "No chance of him diddling that."

Kevin felt hopeful. "So, they, like, stopped. Completely?"

"Yes, and you know what the best part of all this is? Know what he said about her?"

Kevin was a little sceptical. Perhaps he didn't want to hear this part, but he relented. "What?"

"She digs older guys. Much older. Likes them for the experience they have, and the fact the tend to last longer than younger ones. Well, most, anyway."

Kevin felt his spirits raise with this news. *So, maybe she was actually flirting with me, and it wasn't just my imagination.*

Still...

"Man," Kevin said, shaking his head in disbelief. "She is one *hot* little lady."

"I know it's been a while for you," George said. "Quite a while, but what better way to get back into the game than with a young sex starved filly who loves older men? And she has a history of bonking the ones she cleans houses for." George's face was one big smile. "I think you may get a surprise when you get home tonight."

Kevin was doubtful, but felt his pulse quicken at the prospect.

Later, he cut things short with George and headed home. He tried to keep his expectations at zero. But inward, he cursed himself. *I always do this. Get my hopes up. Nothing is going to happen except she'll leave and I'll just whack off as usual.*

He entered his house, and looked around. He found Annette in the kitchen, cleaning up some dishes he had left there to fossilize with yesterday's food. She turned at the sound of him entering, and immediately lit up in a big smile.

"Welcome back," she said, hanging a dishtowel. She leaned against the counter so one hip stuck outward. She looked incredibly sexy that way.

He caught himself staring at her, looking over her lovely form. She didn't seem to mind, in fact she appeared to enjoy his perusal.

"Everything go okay with the cleaning?" he asked.

"Oh, yeah. No problem at all," she locked her gaze onto him. "Just like its owner."

Kevin felt a hard-on start to roar to life in his jeans.

"So," he said.

"So," she said, smiling.

"I meant to ask you, have you had much experience house cleaning before this?" he said, trying to act casual about it.

She frowned a little, making her look all the more appealing. "Yeah, I cleaned a house regularly last summer. Did it for a while. But not anymore."

Well, well, well, he thought. *It is her!* He felt his pulse begin to race.

"Ah, cool," he said.

"I really missed that, too. I really enjoyed it," she said.

"The house?" he said.

"Well, yes, I miss them. But I missed its owner even more," she said, her big blue eyes locked onto his own.

"Why's that?" he almost whispered.

"He'd teach me things. I like to be taught, by older men in particular. Older guys know so many wonderful things."

Suddenly, she closed the distance between them, and put her hands on his shoulders. She was firmly pressed up against him, huge tits mashed against his stomach. Her tummy was also planted firmly against the bulge in his pants, which was growing rapidly.

"Well, you're an older man, more experienced in many things than I," she batted her eyelashes at him. "What would you like to teach me?"

But before he could respond, she kissed him. The smell and taste of her nearly overwhelmed him, but he kissed her back, and with equal passion. Their tongues wrestled, probing the other's mouth.

They necked for several minutes, until she took her hand and grabbed his crotch. He liked it, and ground against her.

Got to get the girl into a bed, and fast, he thought.

His face must of betrayed his thoughts, because Annette said, "I noticed you have a downstairs guest room."

"Yeah," he said.

"Lets fuck there." She grinned wickedly at him.

He liked the way she thought.

She took him by the hand and led him through the house and into the back guest room.

Then, unbidden, she peeled off her t-shirt, revealing her stunningly full cleavage. It was as if her breasts were seconds away from bursting from their confines of the bra.

He stood memorized as she reached back and fiddle with the clasp. She watched him, enjoying his lustful look. Then, she shrugged off the bra and tossed it to the floor.

Her tits were incredible, only sagging slightly now that they were free. Her skin was a beautiful creamy white. Each tit was bigger than his own head. He felt himself start to drool.

Still keeping an eye on his expression, she then wiggled out of her shorts, and thong underwear, tossing those aside, too. She stood before him, completely naked and looking like a Greek Goddess of Fuckability.

She walked forward, breasts jiggling hypnotically, and grabbed at his own shirt. He only flinched just slightly, as if his brain was only now catching up with unfolding events, but he smiled and yielded.

He chuckled and raised his arms so she could pull the it off of him.

Annette ran her hands over his chest, then sucked on one of his nipples, teething it. Then she kissed the other, flicking it with her tongue. He managed to work his hands up between them to cup her ample breasts, squeezing them.

She then grabbed at his belt and undid it with a playful grunt. He smiled and let her work at it. When unbuckled, she unzipped his fly, then squatted down in front of him, pulling his pants down. She managed to work them to his hips, and with one final tug, yanked them down to his knees.

She pulled off his shoes, and then aided him in removing his pants from his ankles. She then turned her attention to the now erect penis in front of her, demanding attention.

Grabbing it eagerly, she stroking it up and down, marvelling at its thickness, and heft. She then put it in her mouth, and started to suck. Looking down at her, all he could see was the back of her head, as she worked her mouth up and down his length with loud slurping gusto.

One of his hands was on the back of her head, holding her ponytail, almost as if to ensure she didn't get away. Slowly stroking him she followed her hands up and down with her mouth, sucking with determination. He really liked it when she partially gagged on his cock.

Up and down she worked him. Long minutes of concentrated effort, with her mouth made his dick glisten, creating a slight foam at its base. Some spit eventually dribbled down to his balls to dangle there.

With one final suck, she kept stroking his shaft, and said, "Let's move to that chair. I want to ride you like a bucking bronco." He eagerly nodded in agreement. She stood, and while guiding him by his dick, gently pulled him over to easy chair in the corner of the room.

She made him sit facing towards her. She placed a hand on either side of his face then she stepped forward a little and pressed his face into her pussy.

He kissed it hungrily, licking and sucking the length of her. She held him there for a very long time, enjoying the sensation. He reached around to grab her round ass cheeks with both hands and squeezed. Occasionally she would grind her pussy in his face, and he enjoyed hearing, and feeling, her moan.

She then turned around and straddled him. Squatting down, she took his dick and guided it inside herself, until she had slid down his full-length. Putting her hands on his thighs, just above the knees, she started to move up and down. He grabbed at her ass while leaning backwards, helping her with the movements.

She rode him, moving slowly at first until she found a wonderful rhythm. Then she started to go faster, always making sure she slid up his entire length, almost until it seemed he would escape her velvety grip, only to suddenly slam down and smack loudly against the flesh of his legs. Many minutes past like this. Riding him on and on.

After a while she switch the position around, so they were facing each other. He smiled at her, as she did so. But his focus quickly switched to her ample breasts. As she slammed up and down, he gripped her tits and sucked and teethed on their nipples. Sometimes he would bury his face between them, until they smothered him. They were so huge!

She looked down at him and said, "I've taught you something, now maybe you can teach me in something in return," she said with a wicked smile.

Again, they switched up positions, this time she knelt on the chair, leaning over it, and he got behind her. Kevin took his hard cock and bounced it playfully off her ass several times. He watched as her buttocks jiggled. Then he guided it down, and very slowly slipped all of it into her waiting pussy. She gasped with the sudden penetration.

Her ass was absolutely perfectly shaped; like a plump inverted heart pressed against his hips. It was so firm, it barely jiggled when he pumped hard against it. He got even more aroused just running his hands around its amazing flesh, over and over.

Her pussy was incredibly slick now, as he had worked her up into a lather. His dick slide in an out of her, causing her pussy to make wet noises. "It's talking to you," she said, looking over her should at him, breathing heavy.

He smacked her ass in response. "I'm teaching it a lesson," he said, smiling.

He pumped her for what seemed like hours, but it was never really long enough. Then he withdrew from her, and turned her around so she was laying partially on the chair, legs outstretched. She smiled up at him, and rubbed at her clit. "Fuck me," she said. "Teach me another lesson!"

He hovered between her widely outstretched legs and suddenly jammed his cock down deep inside her waiting pussy. They both grunted with the roughness of the motion. Then, bracing arms on the chair, he began moving his hips up and down. He pulled himself out almost the full length of his dick, until it nearly unsheathed itself, and then slamming it back down with pleasurable force.

Over and over he did this, getting faster and faster. She moaned with each pelvic thrust. Long wonderful minutes passed as he slammed her pussy again and again. Eventually, the intensity got to be so much Annette's eyes rolled upwards showing only their whites.

Then he slowed, making easy gyrating motions with his hips but could not keep up the relentless pace. With both the feeling of the rubbing wet friction inside her, and seeing her face grimace with the concentrated effort of their passion, he found himself about to orgasm.

"I'm gonna cum!" he finally gasped.

Quickly, Annette pushed him back, unsheathing him from her.

He stood before her, stroking his cock vigorously. Sitting on the edge of the chair, she leaned forward so she could place the bottom of her open mouth against the base of his prick. Her tongue tickled at it eagerly, and her eyes stared up at him with hunger.

He stroked faster, and soon came with a loud moan. His semen spat out all over her; hot squirts into her mouth which slid down her tongue and pooled at the back of her throat. Over her face in long sticky strands that splayed across her cheeks and forehead. In the corner of one eye, down her chin, and he even got some in her hair.

As he sagged with completion, and she made a dramatic show of swallowing.

She smacked her mouth, and rolled her tongue around her lips, getting every white bit. A long thick strand still hung from her chin as she grinned widely at him.

She then grabbed his dick, and sucked it as his erection faded, nursing the last of his load.

He held her head in his hands, feeling the slow motion of her movements, and he grinned up at the ceiling feeling wonderful.

I think I'm going to need a maid more often! He thought.

END

Hot & Horny, Mixer 4
Erotic Mega Bundle
Hardcore Super Pack
Hot & Horny Mega Bundle
Adults Only, Quick & Dirty
Stained Sheets, Quick & Dirty
Filthy Fun, Hot & Horny
Taboo Temptation, Quick & Dirty